I0539620

Contents

Chapter 1: The Threshold

The house breathed differently after survival.

For Keesha Marshall, survival was not a single event but a never-ending process. On the surface, the act of enduring might have seemed simple—barricading the doors, double-locking the windows—but it ran deeper, shaping her every thought. Even now, with Darius King behind bars, she couldn't shake the habit of scanning each room for the faintest whiff of danger. It had become part of how she moved: a sideways glance at the hall before flicking on a light, an involuntary pause whenever she heard a car door slam outside.

Residual Tension

For Keesha, survival meant living with the unrelenting weight of vigilance. Each day brought a fresh onslaught of small reminders that Darius—once capable of warping minds with a whispered phrase—still lurked somewhere in her memories. Though physically jailed, he clung to her psyche like a stain that refused to wash out. Mundane tasks—like brewing coffee or organizing the mail—never felt fully mundane anymore. Every clink of a cup or shuffle of paper carried an undercurrent of possible threat. Would this be the day she found a letter signed by him? A cryptic note that somehow bypassed prison mail censors?

She tried to subdue such fears, reminding herself that it was over—or at least on pause. But her body knew better. Muscles remained tight. Her shoulders constantly tensed, as if anticipating an attack. The ghost of Darius's presence lingered in the chipped corners of walls and in the musty scent of the old carpeting. She'd catch her reflection in the kitchen window at night and feel her heart stutter: Is that me, or something behind me?

No, it was only ever her. But for how long?

The House Remembers

Keesha believed in the idea that spaces held memories—that walls recorded the echoes of past events like grooves in a record. She could still pinpoint the spot on the living room floor where she'd frantically dragged a bookshelf in front of the door, heart hammering in her ears. Her gaze often caught on the odd stain near the baseboard—left after one of Darius's rages had caused her to spill paint in a frantic attempt at covering up damage. Even the kitchen counter she hovered over now had a long scratch where she had once slammed down a knife in terror after hearing what she thought was a break-in.

It wasn't just the physical scars of the house that haunted her, though. At times, the atmosphere itself felt charged. The air turned thick on certain evenings, as if saturated with leftover fear. Shadows seemed to shift in the corners, even when she knew it was just the flicker of an old lightbulb. She wondered how long it would take—months, years—to exorcise Darius's lingering energy from these walls.

Yet, for all its burdens, this house was also their fortress. It had sheltered her and Grace. It had withstood the psychic storms Darius unleashed.

The wavy glass windows and creaking doors had refused to yield, offering them a fragile place of refuge. Sometimes, when the night was calm and the lamplight was warm, the house almost felt like it was breathing in tandem with them, whispering, We made it through.

That was why, despite everything, Keesha still felt love for this battered home. It was a testament to endurance.

Quincy: Protector in the Wings

Across the kitchen, Quincy stood watch. He was a man shaped by discipline—back straight, head on a swivel, his boots silently gripping the linoleum floor. A soldier's instincts lived in him, refusing to let him fully relax. Though he appeared casual in his jeans and a worn T-shirt, Keesha sensed the readiness coiled inside him. Sometimes, she caught him scanning the ceilings or the corners of doorways as if mapping out vantage points or potential chokeholds.

He carried the weight of past deployments— memories of desert nights, the mechanical click of rifles being loaded, the hum of helicopters overhead. That history gave him a unique perspective on fear, on living with the knowledge that an enemy might strike at any moment. He recognized Keesha's thousand-yard stare for what it was: the hallmark of someone who had survived a war at home.

Yet behind Quincy's steeled composure lay a gentle affection, especially for Keesha and Grace. He exuded a quiet vow: I won't let you face danger alone. His protective stance wasn't just about physical security; it was an emotional shield too. After Darius's manipulations, Keesha struggled to trust anyone with her reality. But Quincy had earned a place in her life by standing guard without question, validating her fears without pity.

She took small comfort in the fact that when her own resolve faltered, she could look into Quincy's steady gaze and feel less alone.

Grace at the Center

On the threadbare couch, Grace was deeply engrossed in her drawing. A blanket was draped over her lap, partially hiding the brace she sometimes wore for her scoliosis. Though slender and petite for her age, Grace had a posture that hinted at hard-won resilience. The gentle slope of her spine did little to diminish the determination in her eyes.

Art had become her refuge. The soft scratch of the pencil on paper was a lifeline—an escape from the swirling thoughts that plagued her. Each stroke felt like exhaling a buried fear. A swirl of dark lines might represent the nightmares that haunted her after Darius's psychic intrusions. Sharp angles could be the ramparts she built in her mind to fend off illusions.

She occasionally paused to rub her fingers against her temples, as if warding off a headache or brushing away lingering echoes of Darius's voice. Psychological scars ran deep for her. After all, she had once been a direct conduit for Darius's manipulations; he had used her as a means to torment Keesha, sometimes pushing Grace to say or do things that felt like betrayal. The guilt of those forced actions still gnawed at her, even though she knew she was never truly at fault.

Keesha recognized the flicker of shame that occasionally crossed Grace's face—a memory of times when Darius had twisted her tweener vulnerabilities into weapons. Grace would never say it out loud, but Keesha sensed the girl harbored an ache: What if I hadn't let him in, even by accident? What if I could've resisted more?

No matter how often Keesha reassured her daughter that none of it was her fault, Grace carried that burden silently.

Unspoken Communication

Their eyes met—mother and daughter—and an entire conversation passed in silence. They communicated through micro-expressions, the subtle tilt of a brow, a tiny nod that said I'm okay, are you okay? It was a language birthed from surviving Darius's manipulations, from nights spent huddled together, each afraid to speak too loudly or breathe too heavily.

> We're here, Keesha's gaze said.
> We're strong, Grace's replied.

Even in that moment of connection, a shard of apprehension drove itself between them. Keesha inhaled, steadying her voice. She had to say it; delaying would only give it more power.

> "He's coming out next week."

A hush fell over the small family like a dropped curtain. Quincy's entire frame went rigid, his hand reflexively sliding toward the concealed holster he wore out of habit. Keesha caught the clench of his jaw, the way his breath hissed as he exhaled.

The Name That Haunts

"Darius?"
She nodded. "Darius."

The name was a sickness in the air, tainting it with every possible fear they had tried to bury. Keesha despised how four letters could hold the sum of her nightmares, how even speaking it triggered a surge of anxiety in her chest. She glanced at Grace, saw the pencil quiver in her hand.

In the stillness, Keesha's mind wandered to the first time she had realized Darius wasn't just a smooth-talking manipulator but a psychic predator. How he'd convinced her that she'd misplaced entire conversations, how he subtly rewrote her sense of reality. It had begun so gently—casual references to things she hadn't said, or pointing out that she "forgot" events that never occurred. Then it escalated: illusions, nightmares, forced compliance. Eventually, she found herself questioning if her love for her own child was real, or if he had somehow tampered with that too.

A quiet, sharp terror settled in Keesha's stomach as she remembered those days. For the courts, the case was about "coercion" and "mind games," but those words barely scratched the surface. Darius's capacity to bend reality was monstrous, something the legal system wasn't built to process.

Grace's Reaction

Across the room, Grace gripped her pencil so tightly her knuckles gleamed white. The page beneath bore a half-finished sketch of a dark figure looming in a doorway, arms extended like talons. Keesha's heart twisted at the sight. She wished her daughter could draw happy fields of flowers or the portraits of friends. Instead, Grace's art was dominated by what they feared lurked outside every locked window: shadows that could infiltrate minds as easily as they entered houses.

When Grace's gaze darted up, the raw panic in her eyes was unmistakable. For all the therapy sessions and mental fortifications, for all the times Dr. Flores taught her how to anchor herself—Darius's name could still reduce her to trembling.

"He won't." Keesha said, pressing her palm over Grace's clenched fist. "Not this time. We've learned too much. You've learned too much."

Grace's voice barely rose above a whisper. "What if I'm not strong enough?"

Quincy came closer, his presence solid, a quiet wall of assurance. "You are," he said gently. He didn't touch Grace—afraid to startle her—but the warmth in his voice was palpable. "You're not alone in this."

A tremor passed through Grace, and then she exhaled, letting the pencil roll from her grip onto the couch. "Okay," she murmured, more to herself than anyone else. "Okay."

Battle Plans

It was Keesha who guided them all to the dining table—an old wooden piece she'd inherited from her grandmother. The surface was scarred by coffee rings and half-erased pen marks, yet it served as a makeshift command center. Spread out before them was a map of the neighborhood, dotted with X's where security cameras had been placed, circles indicating areas that might provide vantage points. Yellow sticky notes clung to the edges with scribbled reminders like Check illusions? or Motion sensors?

Leaning over the map, Quincy traced potential entry points with a calloused fingertip. "He'll try to come from the back alley if he wants to be discreet," he said. "But if he's feeling brazen, the front door isn't off the table. The real question is how we protect our minds, not just our walls."

Keesha nodded. "Darius can make you see what isn't there. Or hear things that never happened." Her throat tightened, recalling the nights she spent awake, convinced she heard scratching at the windows. "We need fail-safes. Signals to confirm what's real, what isn't."

Grace's eyes flickered with a haunted memory. She understood too well how easily illusions could erase truth. Once, she'd spent an entire afternoon believing she was trapped in the basement, only to discover she was sitting on her own bed the whole time.

"Maybe I can create a diversion," Grace offered, voice still shaky but tinged with a note of resolve. "Like… illusions of my own. If I draw something—something he'll believe is real—it might distract him long enough for us to figure out what's really happening."

Both Keesha and Quincy looked at her with a blend of admiration and concern. It was a clever idea, but the risk loomed large. If Darius caught on, he would target Grace's mind even more viciously.

"We'll consider it," Keesha said, brushing a hand over Grace's hair. "But your safety comes first."

Hearts on the Table

They pored over the map, discussing everything from mental countermeasures—like repeating code phrases to check if someone was being controlled—to practical steps like reinforcing the basement windows. Quincy suggested rotating watch shifts, but Keesha shook her head. "We still have to live some semblance of a normal life," she murmured, though she knew normalcy was a luxury they might never truly have again.

Yet despite the tension, there was a tangible sense of unity at the table. Each was fighting for something larger than fear: they were fighting for freedom from a man who had once overshadowed their every breath. If survival had been the first step, now they were moving into the realm of defiance.

The Command to Stand Together

At length, the conversation subsided. Night had fully settled outside, the windows reflecting only the dimly lit room. A hush fell, broken by the steady hum of the fridge and the distant chirp of crickets. Keesha stood, arms folded, scanning the map one more time. She felt every day of the last few years pressing down on her: the exhaustion, the heartbreak, the endless cycle of fight-or-flight. But she also felt a renewed determination flaring like a pilot light inside her.

> "No matter what happens," she said, voice tinged with the steel she'd earned, "we don't let him win. Agreed?"

Quincy's nod was almost imperceptible, but the firmness in his eyes said it all: Agreed.

Grace looked at them both. In that instant, she didn't feel like a child overshadowed by her mother or her protector. She felt like an equal, part of a team. Agreed, her eyes said, and a slight tremble in her lip hinted at both anxiety and resolve.

Crossing the Threshold

As they tidied away the map and turned off lights, the house exhaled in the darkness—its old pipes groaning, its floorboards settling. The hush felt significant, like the lull before a storm. Keesha remembered the countless nights she had gone to bed with a stomach full of dread, waiting for a creak in the hallway or a whisper at her door.

But tonight, for the first time in a long while, she felt the smallest flicker of confidence. Perhaps it was the knowledge that she was not alone in her vigil. Quincy was here, calm and watchful. Grace was older, braver, armed with new mental defenses. And the house itself, scarred as it was, had proven it could hold them through the worst of storms.

Before heading to her room, Keesha lingered by the kitchen counter—letting her fingers trace the old scratch that reminded her of darker nights. This time, it felt less like a reminder of trauma and more like a testament to her fortitude: We are still here. We survived.

Somewhere deep in her mind, the fear churned, whispering that Darius's release would test them all again. But that fear no longer stood unchallenged. In its place rose the memory of Grace's unwavering gaze and Quincy's silent promise. They would face this threshold together.

And if the walls still carried echoes of past terrors, they would also witness the forging of something new: a family determined not just to survive, but to reclaim their lives from the man who once held them in psychic bondage.

As the final light clicked off, the darkness wrapped around them—not as an oppressor, but as a canvas upon which their next chapter would be painted. A subtle hush, and the house seemed to whisper in response: We made it before, and we will make it again.

Chapter 2: Preparation

Detective Elena Rodriguez knew from personal experience that justice often slipped through the cracks. She had grown up in a neighborhood where people gave up on the legal system before they were old enough to drive, where corruption and red tape left too many crimes unsolved. Over time, she'd hardened herself to the realities of bureaucratic inertia, resolved to do what she could from within. Still, in all her years on the force, she had never encountered a case like Darius King. The very idea of a man who could manipulate minds—thoughts, memories, even perceptions—seemed pulled from a supernatural thriller rather than police reports.

Yet here she was, flipping through a thick folder of documents detailing Darius's known associates, partial confessions, and transcripts of victim statements that had been painstakingly collected. Many pages contained contradictory accounts from witnesses who swore up and down that Darius was two places at once, or that they remembered events that never occurred. Elena had gleaned one truth from all of it: the law had no language for a psychic predator. They could brand him as a master manipulator, label it "coercion" in the official file, but that was like calling a hurricane a "windy day." It didn't capture the scope of his power.

The Meeting at the Station

She'd called Keesha, Quincy, and Grace for a discreet meeting at the police station after hours. Despite her rank, Elena didn't want too many ears listening in. She trusted only a few colleagues not to balk or roll their eyes at the notion of "mind control." Most would see it as an exaggeration—overly dramatic. But Elena couldn't afford doubt, not when lives were on the line. She respected Keesha's iron will, Quincy's unflinching protection, and the quiet fortitude Grace seemed to radiate even when her hands trembled.

The four of them convened in a small, windowless conference room bathed in the harsh buzz of fluorescent lights. A battered metal table took center stage, its surface scarred by pen marks and coffee rings. The station around them was quiet, the halls mostly empty save for a skeleton crew.

Quincy stood near the door, arms folded, his posture deceptively casual. Elena saw through it; every muscle in his body was taut, ready. Keesha sat to one side, her shoulders tense from what Elena guessed was a potent mix of determination and dread. And across from them both, Grace: a slight figure in an oversized hoodie, face partially hidden by a curtain of hair. The ten year old had a sketchbook perched on the table—an object that Elena suspected was part security blanket, part creative outlet.

Elena cleared her throat. "Thank you for coming," she began, keeping her voice low. "I know it's late, but I wanted to update you on Darius's status. And there are… things I need to share about what he might be planning next."

Her words hung in the stale air. She noted the way Quincy's eyes flitted to the corners of the room, taking stock of possible threats, or perhaps scoping out a quick escape route. Even behind the fortress of police walls, the man was ready to spring into action. A small voice inside Elena applauded that readiness. They needed it.

Broken Systems

Sitting down, Elena placed her thick manila folder on the table. She couldn't help but recall the look of utter exhaustion on the faces of Darius's other victims—people who had come to the police station shaking, eyes rimmed with tears, stammering about experiences they themselves could barely articulate. Some had felt their sanity slip away, manipulated by illusions, by lies inserted into their memories. The system could only offer so much: restraining orders, psychological counseling, and eventually, in Darius's case, a prison sentence. But how do you keep a psychic behind bars if he can continue to manipulate minds remotely?

> "He'll be watching," Elena said, flipping open the folder. "He's got connections—inside, outside. Even behind bars, his influence extends. I've interviewed corrections officers who swear they're seeing double, or having lapses in judgment they can't explain. He's planning his next move right now, I guarantee it."

At that, Keesha leaned forward, hands splayed on the tabletop. Elena could see the tension around the woman's mouth, the crow's feet etched into her eyes that spoke of many sleepless nights. "Then we make moves he doesn't see coming," Keesha said. There was a trembling passion in her voice, underpinned by the ferocity of a mother protecting her child.

Elena nodded in acknowledgment. "That's exactly why I wanted to speak with you privately. We need to form a plan that his usual tactics can't dismantle."

Threads of Alliance

An uneasy silence settled for a moment. Grace fiddled with the corner of one of her medical files that lay open in front of her, revealing extensive records: heart transplant details, scoliosis surgeries, and repeated hospital stays. Elena found herself thinking of the internal strength it must have taken for Grace to survive all that—and then endure Darius's psychic manipulations on top of it.

After a moment, Grace shut the file with a soft click. A pen on the table twitched, rolling a few inches. The movement was so small that Elena almost dismissed it, but Quincy's darting gaze confirmed he'd seen it too. The detective's brow furrowed. "What was that?"

Keesha opened her mouth, hesitated, then looked to her daughter. Grace nodded, and the mother spoke. "Something started happening after her heart transplant," she said, voice tight. "At first, it was minor stuff—like Grace knowing things before they happened, or little items shifting places. We can't fully explain it, but it's more pronounced when she's stressed. She can… move objects. Sense thoughts, sometimes."

Elena felt a flicker of shock. She'd heard rumors—whispers about Grace possibly having some psychic or telekinetic ability. But hearing it confirmed was different. Her mind reeled with the implications: Could Grace block Darius's intrusions? Or would her abilities make her even more vulnerable? She glanced at Quincy, whose jaw was set in a protective line.

> "That's why we're cautious," Quincy said grimly. "If Darius learns about this, he'll come for her first. He might see it as a challenge or a tool he could twist."

Elena drummed her fingers on the folder, scanning the tension in their faces. She felt a strange surge of hope. Maybe Grace's abilities could tip the scales. "It could also be a game-changer," she said carefully. "A way to fight him on his own terms."

Grace's eyes lifted, their hazel depths reflecting a swirl of fear and subdued resolve. "I'm tired of being scared," she murmured. "I want to be the one who stands up to him… instead of running."

Detective's Concern

Elena recognized the bravery in that statement. At the same time, a pang of worry gnawed at her. If Grace was still discovering her powers, any confrontation with Darius might risk pushing her over the edge—like an untrained fighter stepping into the ring with a seasoned champion. Yet the detective also saw that Grace had already survived more trauma than most adults. If anyone could find the internal fortitude to face Darius head-on, it might be this slight, determined ten year old.

"Look," Elena said, exhaling, "I've been tracing Darius's movements for years. Even before he landed in prison, he cultivated a network of… devotees, for lack of a better term. People who believe in his psychic gifts, who'd do anything he asks. We've identified a few, but there are likely more. If he calls on them, you could face threats from multiple angles, not just him."

Quincy nodded. "So our plan has to account for potential proxies. He might not show up himself at first. He'll send pawns or illusions."

"That's right." Elena's finger tapped a bulleted list on the folder. "Known associates: one named Travis Warren, a woman named Roberta King—distant cousin, apparently—and a handful of others who aren't fully confirmed. They'll be watching you, looking for weaknesses. That means everything you do, from grocery shopping to doctor appointments, might be under scrutiny."

Keesha's face tightened. "So we hide like fugitives? That's not living."

Elena softened her tone. "I don't want you living in fear. But I need you to be smart. Darius thrives on scaring people into making mistakes."

A brief hush followed. In it, Elena sensed the shared resolve in the room, an unspoken vow that Darius would not break them again.

Digging Deeper

They spent the next hour discussing practical defenses. Elena shared what she knew about combating psychological manipulation: grounding techniques, signals to confirm reality with one another, a system of code words. Quincy chimed in with suggestions for physical security—cameras, motion detectors, secure phone lines. Keesha took notes, expression grim but determined, occasionally pausing to rub Grace's shoulder when the girl's face grew too tense.

All the while, Grace's pencil scratched over her notebook. At first, Elena thought she was doodling to self-soothe, but when she glanced at the open pages, she saw intricate sketches of labyrinths, swirling shapes, and shadowy figures. In one corner, a small flame stood alone, surrounded by curling black lines. Elena's stomach tightened at the sight, struck by how it seemed to encapsulate their entire struggle: a tiny light threatened by an ever-encroaching dark.

> "We need to find ways to fight him that he doesn't anticipate," Keesha said, her voice steady despite the weight of the conversation. "He feeds on fear and confusion. But we've learned. He won't catch us off guard again."

Elena studied the woman's face, etched with resilience that came from having her reality dismantled and pieced back together. She admired Keesha's courage more than she could say. "I agree," Elena said. "We use every resource—official and unofficial—to keep him boxed in."

Tensions and Truths

Suddenly, the lights flickered. It was just a brief surge, common in the older building, but everyone stiffened. Quincy's hand drifted near his sidearm. Grace's breath caught, her eyes darting around the room. Elena felt her own pulse spike. For a heartbeat, they all wondered if it was Darius somehow reaching out from behind bars.

But the lights steadied, and the tense moment passed. Elena cleared her throat, trying to dispel the lingering dread. "Another thing," she said. "Darius's next parole hearing—despite everything—is on the horizon. If the system fails, if some legal technicality arises… we have to be prepared to act."

Keesha looked ill at the thought. "He can't walk free. He just can't."

"We'll do our best to make sure that doesn't happen," Elena promised, though she knew how fragile that promise was. "But if it does, you'll need to be ready."

The detective felt the gravity settle again. This trio—Keesha, Quincy, and Grace—had been thrown into a nightmare scenario. Yet she saw, in each of them, a core of defiance that refused to be snuffed out. Quincy's brand of defiance was stoic vigilance; Keesha's was maternal fierceness; Grace's was creative resilience. Elena found herself unexpectedly moved by their unity.

Final Words of Resolve

At last, the clock on the wall showed that midnight was close. Elena stretched out her shoulders, acutely aware of how drained she felt. She snapped the folder shut, offering them a grim, yet earnest smile. "You've got a tough road," she said, echoing her earlier sentiment. "But if there's a group that can stand against Darius, it's you. You've been in his darkness before, and you found a way out."

Keesha stood, lifting her own stack of notes. "We did," she said quietly. "And this time, we won't just survive. We'll end it."

Something in her tone suggested a willingness to cross moral lines if that was what it took. Elena understood—she'd seen victims forced into corners where their only options were desperate. The detective hoped, for everyone's sake, that it wouldn't come to that.

> "Remember," she said, turning to Grace. "Sometimes strength isn't just about wielding power. It's about timing and strategy—knowing when to act and when to retreat."

Grace met Elena's gaze with unwavering eyes. She said nothing, but the quiet determination on her face spoke volumes. The young girl was done being a victim; she was determined to become an active participant in ending Darius's reign of terror. Her slender shoulders trembled with both fear and a fierce kind of courage. It reminded Elena that, beneath all this talk of psychic warfare and covert planning, Grace was still a young person forced to grow up too soon.

With final nods and subdued farewells, they gathered their belongings. Quincy held the door open, scanning the corridor before motioning the others through. Elena followed them, switching off the conference room lights behind her. The hallway beyond was dim, the faint hum of vending machines and overhead lamps the only sounds. The entire station felt half-asleep, as though it sensed the storm swirling around them.

As the trio left the station, Elena lingered a moment, watching their silhouettes vanish down the hallway. She felt an odd mixture of protectiveness and caution. Darius was no ordinary criminal; he was a living nightmare, a viper that could slither into minds. Yet something about these three gave her hope. They weren't just victims. They were survivors who had banded together, forging their own brand of unwavering loyalty.

A Private Reflection

Alone in the corridor, Elena rubbed her temples, a headache threatening behind her eyes. She recalled the earliest days of investigating Darius King—when she'd first tried to gather credible evidence of his "supernatural" powers. She'd lost sleep second-guessing every detail: Could he really do this? Am I losing my mind too? But the testimonies were too consistent, too raw to dismiss. If she'd learned one thing, it was that underestimating Darius was a mistake with deadly consequences.

But now, after hours of planning with Keesha, Quincy, and Grace, Elena found herself harboring a small but potent sense of optimism. Perhaps Grace's newfound abilities—whatever they truly were—could provide the edge they needed. And the determination in Keesha's eyes was a force in its own right.

Elena finally pushed away from the wall, heading to her desk to type up fresh notes. There was no guarantee any official tactic would hold Darius once he decided to move, but she would do everything in her power to fortify these people who'd become more than just a case file. She'd stand by them, through every legal or extralegal means at her disposal.

Because—she acknowledged grimly—the fight had already begun. It was no longer looming on the horizon. It was here, in the station's flickering lights, in Grace's trembling fingers, and in the maps and codes they'd just devised. They weren't waiting for Darius to pounce. They were preparing to face him head-on, each carrying scars that told the story of why they simply could not lose this time.

And if that meant crossing lines or rewriting the rules to safeguard Keesha, Quincy, and Grace, Detective Elena Rodriguez would do it without hesitation. After all, some threats demanded more than a well-crafted legal argument. Some battles required a shield forged by people who understood what it meant to fight for one another's sanity and souls.

As the clock struck midnight, Elena wondered if Darius felt the same shift in the air—if he sensed that his old victims were no longer cornered prey, but a determined force gathering its strength. She allowed herself a final moment of hope before logging into the station's computer to continue her preparations.

Chapter 3: The Birthday Trap

Balloons and colorful streamers lined the living room, their cheerful brightness clashing against a thrumming tension that crackled in the air. The smell of vanilla cake and grilled appetizers mingled awkwardly with the acrid undercurrent of dread. Neighbors and friends circulated in polite clusters, trying their best to pretend everything was normal. Yet there was no ignoring the man by the refreshment table— Darius King, newly released from prison.

Disquiet Under the Decorations

Keesha stood near a side table, half-hidden behind an arrangement of birthday cards for Grace. She wore a light sweater and jeans, an outfit chosen to project a calm she didn't feel. Her pulse hammered, and she couldn't shake the sense that every balloon and streamer was a mask of normalcy, barely concealing the predator in the room.

She scanned the faces of the guests:

- Mr. Morales, the neighbor who once helped fix their fence, now eyeing Darius with obvious unease.
- Cynthia, Keesha's coworker, fiddling with her phone as if desperate for a distraction.
- A couple of Grace's school friends, hugging cups of soda, unsure whether to laugh or flee when Darius looked their way.

Keesha forced a tight smile at the guests who offered half-hearted birthday wishes. They have no idea what they've stumbled into, she thought grimly. If they understood how dangerous Darius truly was, most of them would have run for the door the moment he arrived.

Grace's Vigil and Inner Turmoil

On an oversized armchair near the corner, Grace curled into herself, arms clasped around her legs. The day was supposed to be about her—celebrating another year of life. Yet the presence of her father turned the occasion into a showdown. Her hazel eyes followed him with an intensity bordering on fear, but also something else: a defiance that had grown in her since the last time he'd tried to control her mind.

In her lap rested a sketchbook, open to a half-finished piece. If anyone peered close enough, they'd see dark lines forming the shape of a labyrinth, surrounded by tall, spindly figures. Each figure had elongated fingers, reaching inward. At the center was a tiny, glowing shape—perhaps a candle or a heart. Grace had been drawing it all morning, hoping to exorcise the anxiety that clung to her like a second skin.

Every so often, her pencil tapped the paper in a staccato beat, matching the rapid flutter of her heartbeat. She wondered if she'd ever know a birthday without tension, without the looming shadow of Darius. This year, she promised herself, things will be different.

Quincy's Calculated Ruse

Across the room, leaning against the kitchen counter, Quincy looked for all the world like he'd had one too many beers. His eyelids drooped, his shoulders slouched, and he slurred a greeting to a couple of neighbors who passed by. But Keesha knew better: this display was an elaborate act, bolstered by a carefully dosed sedative—enough to mimic drunkenness while keeping him on edge. His posture might appear lax, but she recognized the tension in his jaw, the alertness in his gaze.

He had volunteered for this role without hesitation. "I'll be the easy target," he'd said, flashing a wry smile. Beneath that self-effacing humor lay a resolute core: if Darius tried to use his abilities on Quincy, better Quincy than Grace or Keesha. At least Quincy had trained himself to withstand mental strain—he'd spent time in the military learning resilience, though even he'd never faced a psychic threat like Darius.

From her vantage, Keesha could see Quincy's hand twitch near his waistband. He was ready. If Darius made a move—any move—Quincy would react.

The Predator Among Them

And then there was Darius King himself, standing near a table laden with sandwiches and a half-finished punch bowl. He wore a casual blazer over a crisp shirt, exuding a magnetic charm. A low murmur spread among guests who glanced at him sidelong, uncertain whether to greet him or avoid him. Some recognized him only as the "ex-husband" or "the father," but Keesha suspected a few had heard whispers of darker rumors—though not the full truth.

Darius's presence felt like static electricity in the air, a hum that set everyone's nerves on edge. Even those who didn't know his history seemed unsettled, as though they sensed an undercurrent of danger emanating from him. Every so often, he'd catch Keesha's eye and offer a languid smile that made her stomach twist.

His gaze often flicked to Grace, and each time, a jolt of anger spiked through Keesha. She hated the way he looked at their daughter, as though he still owned her—some twisted fatherly claim that had nothing to do with genuine love. In truth, Keesha believed Darius was here not to celebrate Grace, but to taunt them all. A quiet vow simmered in her mind: We're not playing your game anymore.

The Trap Set in Motion

They had orchestrated this confrontation with Detective Elena Rodriguez, who waited outside in an unmarked car. It was risky, inviting Darius to a gathering of friends and neighbors, but Keesha had insisted: "He'll come if he thinks we're vulnerable." And come he did, strolling in with a brazen confidence that the legal system couldn't hold him. Wrong, Keesha thought grimly.

Grace tried to steady her breathing. Their plan hinged on letting Darius believe he still held the upper hand until it was too late. Her eyes flicked to the watch on her wrist. At exactly 8:45 PM, Keesha would send a pre-scheduled text alert to Rodriguez. Fifteen minutes to go.

Darius Makes His Move

Finally, Darius clinked a spoon against his glass of whiskey, the crystalline sound cutting through the low buzz of conversation. All eyes turned toward him. Keesha felt the air tense, as if the entire room inhaled at once.

> "Ladies and gentlemen," Darius began, smiling broadly. "A toast! To Grace, our birthday girl."

He raised his glass, then turned to Grace. Keesha caught the subtle narrowing of his eyes. There was a predatory glint there, a challenge.

> "May she grow up strong, beautiful… and far wiser than her dear mother."

A ripple of unease passed through the crowd. A few polite claps followed, but several guests exchanged questioning looks. Why would a father toast his daughter with such a pointed jab at her mother?

Keesha's fists curled at her sides, nails biting into her palms. She forced herself to project a thin, polite smile. Inside, every nerve sizzled with fury. Grace shrank back in her seat, hugging her sketchbook tighter.

Tension on Display

The hush became suffocating. Darius placed his glass on a nearby table. "Grace, come here, sweetheart," he said, voice silk-smooth. "I've got something… special for you."

The air felt charged with an unspoken threat. Grace hesitated, fear etched in her eyes. No one else moved. A few neighbors glanced at each other, unsure if this was some family drama they should politely ignore. The sense of anticipation was almost unbearable.

When Grace didn't budge, Darius's facade slipped, irritation flitting across his face. Then he smiled again, turning to the room at large. "Let's liven this party up, shall we?"

Without warning, he pointed to a timid accountant named Rafael standing by the fireplace.

> "You. Dance," Darius commanded, his tone thick with something more than mere suggestion.

Rafael blinked. "I… don't—"

"Dance."

Suddenly, it was as if strings pulled Rafael's limbs. He began a jerky, unnatural jig, eyes wide with confusion and mortification. Nervous laughter flitted through the room, but it quickly turned to horror as people realized this wasn't just a silly party trick. Something about Rafael's face—the terror in his eyes—gave away that he couldn't stop himself.

Quincy, still feigning intoxication, stirred. His jaw flexed, fists itching to intervene. But the plan required waiting for the precise moment, the one that would fully expose Darius.

Demonstrations of Power

Darius, drunk on his own abilities, singled out a teenage girl next. With a lazy gesture, he forced her to crawl on all fours, eyes unfocused. The guests murmured in alarm, some stepping forward as if to help, only to recoil at the sense of unreality that gripped the room. Is this real? More than one person rubbed their eyes or shook their head, disbelieving the sight.

Keesha's stomach clenched. This was the side of Darius she knew too well—the domineering psychic who derived pleasure from humiliating others. She wanted to scream at him to stop, but she had to maintain the trap. Just a few more minutes. She glanced at the clock on the wall: 8:43 PM.

Grace, trembling, watched in horror. Part of her remembered being on the receiving end of that power—Darius puppeteering her, making her walk or speak against her will. A swirl of anger flared within her. She pressed her pencil into the sketchbook so hard that the lead snapped.

The Queen Sacrifices a Pawn

Across the room, a few defiant souls tried to snap their neighbors out of the bizarre compulsion, shaking shoulders or calling names. But Darius merely laughed, a cold, cruel sound. Each time someone tried to intervene, a flick of his hand made them hesitate, as if an invisible weight pressed on their minds. He turned his attention back to Grace, eyes gleaming with twisted triumph.

> "Sweetheart," he cooed, "would you like to join us? Or shall I make you?"

Grace's heart thundered. She shot a glance toward Keesha, then at Quincy. Both nodded almost imperceptibly. They were ready. They had to spring the trap now, before Darius went too far or hurt someone beyond repair.

Keesha stepped forward, squaring her shoulders. She made her voice ring across the stilled, horrified crowd. "You've always been the life of the party, Darius."

He turned to her, arching an eyebrow. "Oh, Keesha," he murmured, a mix of condescension and nostalgia in his tone. "Still trying to save every lost cause, including yourself?"

She swallowed the rage rising in her throat. "You've been drinking, haven't you? I can see it in your eyes."

Darius smirked, brandishing his whiskey glass. "What if I have?" He took another swig. "I'm celebrating my return to freedom, after all."

Keesha's lips curled in a grim, tight smile. "I thought you might." Her gaze swept the table of liquor bottles. "That's why I made sure they were… specially prepared."

For the first time that night, Darius's confidence faltered. A flicker of uncertainty crossed his face. "What did you do?"

"Call it a little chemical insurance," Keesha said softly. "Something to disrupt your focus. Let's see you control people now."

All around the room, the guests who had been enslaved by Darius's commands began regaining control of their bodies. The man forced to dance stumbled to a halt, gasping. The teenage girl blinked, tears rushing to her eyes as her mind cleared. A wave of confusion and outrage swept the crowd, many staring at Darius with dawning fury.

The Clock Strikes 8:45

Across the room, Keesha discreetly tapped SEND on her phone. At 8:45 PM, a scheduled text flew to Detective Rodriguez's line outside. Within seconds, the lights of police vehicles began to flicker through the windows.

A murmur of alarm spread through the guests, some stepping back, others pressing forward to see what was happening. Blue and red lights danced across the walls, an eerie contrast to the party decorations.

Darius stumbled, panic edging into his features. He turned, realizing his hold was slipping and the crowd was shifting from fearful to angry.

The front door burst open: Detective Rodriguez, flanked by uniformed officers, swept into the living room. The tension snapped into chaos. People shrieked; neighbors pressed themselves against walls to make room for the police.

> "Darius King," Rodriguez called, voice echoing. "You're under arrest!"

Showdown and Collapse

Darius tried one last time to use his power. He lunged toward a cluster of guests, eyes narrowed, willing them to shield him or create a diversion. But the drug Keesha had mixed into the liquor dulled his psychic edge, leaving only a fraction of his usual prowess. The crowd began to recoil, no longer enthralled by him.

A flicker of raw fury crossed his face. He turned on Keesha, snarling, "You think this changes anything? I'm not finished with you!"

Quincy shoved off the counter, his "drunken" act vanishing. In two swift strides, he intercepted Darius before he could reach Keesha. Even with Darius's powers weakened, Quincy stayed vigilant—he half expected illusions or mind-bending tricks. Instead, Darius lashed out physically, a wild punch connecting clumsily with Quincy's shoulder.

Quincy's reflexes kicked in. He blocked another swing, twisted Darius's arm behind his back. The man who had so often wielded invisible power now found himself physically pinned.

Rodriguez's officers surged forward, cuffing him as he spat insults and accusations. One officer read Darius his rights over his garbled protests, while another steadied him. His voice cut through the room, venomous: "You can't do this! I'm untouchable!"

Relief in the Aftermath

By then, the party guests had recovered enough to realize Darius's downfall was real. A few stared in shock, hugging each other or murmuring to the officers about how they'd felt used, manipulated. One older neighbor, tears streaming, said she swore she'd never come to a birthday party again. The atmosphere pulsed with a combination of anger, relief, and the surreal sense of having witnessed something beyond the ordinary.

In the midst of it all, Grace stood up from the armchair, trembling. Her sketchbook slipped from her lap, pages fluttering. She walked unsteadily toward Keesha, sidestepping the police as they hauled Darius to his feet. His wrathful gaze slid to Grace, and for a moment, her heart twinged with the old fear that he could still reach her mind.

But he didn't. He merely glowered, helpless in the officers' grip.

> "Mom," Grace whispered, voice shaking with adrenaline. "Is it… over?"

Keesha pulled her daughter into a tight embrace, pressing her cheek to Grace's hair. "Yes," she breathed, though a part of her remained cautious—Darius had a way of rearing back when least expected. Still, in this moment, he was powerless.

Candles and Wishes

Outside, the swirl of police lights illuminated the front yard. A pair of ambulances arrived just in case anyone needed medical attention after Darius's forced humiliations. Inside, the living room still bore the remnants of streamers and half-eaten cake, an incongruous backdrop to the scene of an arrest.

Detective Rodriguez caught Keesha's eye and gave a small nod of affirmation: We did it. Keesha nodded back, tears threatening to spill. The plan had worked—risky, but successful.

As Darius was led away, cursing and thrashing, the cluster of remaining guests parted like the Red Sea, scowling at him. A hush fell once the police cars vanished down the street. People murmured about going home, about calling loved ones. Others quietly approached Keesha and Grace, offering shaky hugs, relief, or uncertain words of support.

In the middle of the wrecked party, Grace turned to the birthday cake, which still waited on the table, its candles unlit. She glanced at Keesha and Quincy. Though her hands trembled, she lit the candles herself, one by one, creating a halo of gentle light in the darkened room.

Her voice was soft, still threaded with nerves, as she said, "Mom, can we… can we just do this? Please?"

Keesha nodded, tearful and proud. "Of course."

Grace gazed at the modest flames dancing atop the cake. Despite the chaos of the evening, this was her birthday—her moment to reclaim something that Darius had tried to overshadow. Quincy quietly joined them, resting a supportive hand on Grace's shoulder.

"Make a wish," he said gently.

Grace inhaled, the hush returning. She closed her eyes, visualizing a future no longer dominated by fear or dread, a life where she and Keesha could breathe without second-guessing every shadow. Then she blew out the candles, sending a faint spiral of smoke toward the ceiling.

Her wish was simple: freedom.

Epilogue to the Night

In the aftermath, a few guests lingered to help clean up, moving with hushed voices as though they didn't want to disturb the fragile peace that had been won. The balloons still bobbed cheerfully, oblivious to the drama that had played out beneath them. Slowly, people trickled out, offering Keesha and Grace concerned hugs or murmured thanks that the truth had finally been laid bare.

When at last the house stood mostly empty— only Keesha, Grace, Quincy, and a couple of close friends left—Keesha realized how exhausted she was. The tension that had fueled her all night began to drain, leaving her limbs heavy and her mind buzzing.

Grace sank back into the armchair, hugging the sketchbook to her chest. She didn't bother finishing the half-drawn labyrinth. She had a strange sense that this was a chapter closing. Outside, the distant hum of sirens faded, replaced by the chirp of crickets in the warm summer night.

Quincy approached, the sedation wearing off, and squeezed Grace's shoulder gently. "You did good, kid," he said, voice low. "You stood your ground."

Grace mustered a small smile. She felt like she'd aged a year in one night. "We did it... together."

Keesha joined them, pulling both into a loose embrace. She closed her eyes, exhaling the last of her pent-up fear. "No more birthdays with him looming over us," she whispered. "Next year will be different, Grace. I promise."

Looking Ahead

Outside, red and blue lights still flashed faintly at the end of the block, where police officers took statements from rattled neighbors. But inside, a quiet peace settled. They had faced the wolf in their midst and, for once, emerged triumphant. Yet Keesha knew the fight wasn't fully over. Darius had a way of sowing chaos even from behind bars.

Still, for tonight—on Grace's birthday—they had won a crucial battle. The trap had been laid, the line had been crossed, and Darius had fallen into their snare. As she dimmed the living room lights and urged Grace to get some rest, Keesha allowed herself a moment of relief. She looked at the half-eaten birthday cake, at the scattered plates and cups, at the discarded balloons swaying gently from the ceiling. He's gone—for now, she reminded herself. We've taken one giant step.

In the dim glow of a single lamp, mother and daughter shared a final glance, an unspoken promise that they'd reclaim their lives from the man who had once twisted their world into a nightmare. Grace whispered a quiet goodnight and disappeared into her bedroom, her shoulders still trembling but her spirit unbroken.

The house exhaled softly, the tension easing from its walls. And in that hush, Keesha allowed herself one small victory: Darius might try again, but they weren't the same frightened family he once controlled. They had changed— stronger, more united, and ready to defend the peaceful future Grace deserved.

Chapter 4: Possession

Shadows and Storm Warnings

Well before sunset, dark clouds rolled across the sky, piling up like a looming threat on the horizon. The air turned thick, and the temperature dropped noticeably. Inside Keesha Marshall's home, every creak, every subtle flicker of the lights, felt like an omen. She couldn't shake the sensation that Darius King—supposedly behind bars—still hovered at the edges of her awareness, like an unwelcome presence haunting the periphery of her mind.

In the cramped living room, the silhouettes of old family photos flickered in and out of the half-light, shapes dancing as the storm outside toyed with the power supply. Even the beams of the ceiling seemed to groan under the pressure of the impending thunderhead. Keesha tried to steady her breathing, reminding herself that Darius was locked up. But is he really gone? whispered a voice at the back of her mind.

Grace's Vigil

Near the front window, Grace stood with her arms crossed protectively over her chest. She wore a hoodie a size too large, its sleeves pulled down to her knuckles—a small shield against the creeping dread. The lamplight revealed a tension in her posture that no ten year old should bear.

Detective Elena Rodriguez had dropped by earlier with more unsettling news: Darius's lawyers were exploiting legal technicalities, pushing for an appeal or a new hearing.

Bureaucratic slip-ups at the prison might give him leverage. To Keesha and Grace, the justice system felt like a sieve that could never properly contain a man who could manipulate minds.

But the legal battle was only the surface. Deeper, intangible dangers lurked—the psychic infiltration that Darius had mastered. If he found any crack in Grace's mental defenses, he could puppeteer her thoughts, twist her into his weapon again.

Standing by the window, Grace peered out into the swirling dusk. Lightning flashed in the distance, illuminating the street in harsh, white bursts. She couldn't name the feeling, but it was as if something called to her from the storm. A chill raced down her spine. He's near. Even if he's not physically here, he's near.

Building the Fortresses Within

Since childhood, Grace had wrestled with psychic echoes—first from Darius's manipulations, and later from her own budding abilities. Under Dr. Miriam Flores's guidance, she learned to envision her mind as a vast fortress. She'd seal each door and window in that mental stronghold, telling herself: He can't come in unless I let him.

These exercises were grueling. Keesha often found her daughter trembling afterward, cheeks flushed with effort and tears in her eyes. "It's like trying to hold a flood back with a single sandbag," Grace confessed more than once. "He's so angry whenever he can't break through… like he's banging on the walls, trying to claw his way in."

When Keesha held Grace's hands during these moments, she felt the tension thrumming in every tendon of the tween's slender wrists. She wished she could fight Darius on Grace's behalf, dive into those psychic depths and expel him for good. But this was Grace's battle more than anyone's. She was the one whose mind Darius coveted as a vantage point.

A Tense Evening Ritual

As the storm intensified, thunder rattled the windows. Quincy moved from room to room, systematically double-checking locks, pulling curtains tight. His background as a soldier never left him; vigilance was second nature. Usually, he'd offer some wry reassurance— We'll make it through the night. But tonight, he barely spoke. Tension pulled at the corners of his mouth as he considered the possibility that Darius might have manipulated guards or influenced parole officers.

Outside, wind lashed the shrubs. Raindrops spattered the windows in a rising clamor. A sense of approaching doom settled over the house. Keesha brewed coffee she didn't really want, just for the comforting smell. She caught Grace's eye, saw the swirl of fear there, and tried to give an encouraging nod. Even that small gesture felt forced.

Rodriguez hovered near the kitchen doorway, her phone periodically lighting up with updates from the station. She scanned each incoming text, expression growing more rigid as new information arrived. The detective's palm pressed over her phone as though bracing for the worst.

At last, the phone buzzed decisively. She glanced down, reading the message. Her face drained of color. Keesha froze, heart pounding. This is it. Something's happened.

The Escape

Rodriguez lifted her gaze, meeting Keesha's eyes. A grim hush settled. "He's escaped," she said, her voice tight with controlled urgency. "They say he's armed and dangerous. No details yet on how… but we have to assume he's coming here."

For a moment, Keesha's vision tunneled. The floor seemed to tilt beneath her feet. "No," she whispered, but the word sounded hollow. Fear flared so sharply that she could hardly breathe. She looked to Grace, whose face reflected the same dread. The tween clutched the windowsill as if it were the only thing keeping her upright.

Quincy's posture went from tense to coiled readiness. He quietly unholstered his sidearm, checking it with practiced efficiency. "We hold this position," he said, voice low. "We don't panic. We're prepared."

Outside, lightning split the sky, illuminating the street in jagged lines of brilliance. The howl of sirens grew closer, echoing in the swirling wind. It felt like nature itself joined the alarm, screaming a warning: Darius is free.

Gathering Storm

As if on cue, the house lights flickered. Thunder boomed loud enough to rattle picture frames off the wall. Keesha fought to keep her composure, scanning for any sign of forced entry. But the door remained latched, the windows locked. Still, a nagging voice insisted: He doesn't need doors or windows to get in. Not if he can slip into our minds.

Then Grace gasped, doubling over with a hand pressed to her forehead. "He's here," she rasped. "I can feel him… he's trying to—" She broke off, breathing heavily. A wave of cold washed over the living room, or at least it felt that way, as though the temperature had dropped ten degrees in seconds.

Quincy rushed to her side, supporting her with one arm. "Stay with us, kid," he murmured. "Focus on the fortress. Shut him out."

Grace closed her eyes, brow furrowed in concentration. For a moment, it seemed as if she might push his presence back. Then the front door slammed inward.

The Fatal Mistake

The front door, locked just moments ago, smashed open as though struck by a violent gust. Wind and rain burst inside, drenching the entryway. And there stood Darius King—soaked, eyes wide with a manic fire. His hair was plastered to his skull, and a twisted grin contorted his features. He looked more feral than civilized, a cornered predator who refused to submit.

Keesha's stomach plummeted. He was supposed to be safely behind bars. Yet here he was in the flesh, defying every restraint the law had tried to place on him. Thunder rumbled overhead, the storm's fury matching the turmoil in the living room.

Quincy lifted his weapon, stepping protectively in front of Keesha and Grace. "Don't move!" he commanded, voice steady despite the adrenaline coursing through him. Behind him, Rodriguez shouted into her radio, calling for immediate backup. The swirl of sirens outside intensified, lights flashing down the street.

But Darius merely sneered. "You think bullets can stop me? Bars can't hold me, and neither can you." He extended his empty hands, showing he carried no firearm. Yet everyone in the room knew his true weapon wasn't physical.

Keesha saw his gaze fix on Grace, and her heart lurched. She knew what he intended: if he could seize Grace's mind again, he could vanish into her body, slip away in the confusion, and continue his reign of terror from within.

> "You'll never lock me up again," Darius growled, voice cutting through the thunderclap. "I'll find the safest place to hide."

Grace stumbled back, fear etched into her face, but the spark of defiance in her eyes hadn't died. She heard Keesha shout, "Stay away from her!" but she could barely register it over the roaring in her ears. Lightning flashed, illuminating Darius's feral grin as he lunged forward.

A Desperate Shot

Quincy fired, the recoil kicking his shoulder. The bullet went wide, lodging in the wall. Instinct had made him aim for a nonlethal shot, but Keesha's scream made him hesitate—she didn't want Grace anywhere near that gunfire if Darius forced her to move.

Darius took advantage of the momentary confusion, unleashing a psychic assault aimed directly at Grace. The ten year old felt a vicious pressure slamming into her consciousness, like a tidal wave trying to drown her mind. Her breath caught in her throat, and for an instant, she feared she'd be lost under the force of his will.

The Instant of Inversion

Time seemed to freeze. Keesha's ears rang with the echo of thunder, sirens, and her own pounding heart. She watched in horror as Grace's back arched, eyes going wide. Darius's face contorted with concentration—his pupils dilated, sweat rolling down his temples. He was pouring every ounce of his psychic power into overtaking Grace's mind.

Keesha clenched her fists, feeling helpless. "No," she whispered, tears threatening to spill. Memories of the last time he'd seized Grace, how he'd forced her to say things that broke Keesha's heart, swarmed her thoughts. Not again. Please, not again.

But this time, something shifted. Grace had prepared. She'd built her mental fortress, and the moment she felt Darius's presence pushing into her mind, she pulled instead of resisting. It was an audacious strategy, one Dr. Flores had tentatively proposed—If he tries to get in, you take his momentum and yank him into your domain.

For a heartbeat, the air shimmered, charged with psychic energy. Even the static-laced radio chatter seemed to hush. Then Keesha sensed a wave of invisible force, as if gravity had turned sideways.

Grace's eyes flared with determination. She reversed the psychic current mid-lunge. Darius's expression changed from predatory to stunned as his consciousness tumbled forward, no longer lodging in Grace but crashing inward like a fish snared in a net.

A Reversal of Power

They both stumbled. Darius let out a gasp that turned into a silent scream. Grace's face twisted in fierce resolve—she was holding him, not letting him slip free. In that moment, it felt like the entire room quivered. Quincy and Rodriguez watched with wide eyes, uncertain whether to intervene or stand back.

Then both Grace and Darius collapsed to their knees, trembling. Keesha surged forward, but Quincy held her back, wary of interfering in a psychic struggle he barely understood. For a breathless instant, no one moved.

Suddenly, Grace's body jerked, eyes flying open. Simultaneously, Darius's body—the man kneeling—blinked in confusion. Keesha felt the air release, as though a massive bubble had burst. It took her a moment to realize what had happened: Grace had succeeded in reversing the possession.

The Swap

The tall figure wearing Darius's face rose unsteadily, turning to Keesha with tears in his eyes. "Mom?" The voice was deeper, jarring in its timbre, but the intonation was unmistakably Grace. Keesha's heart twisted, a mix of relief and heartbreak flooding her.

Across from them, the smaller, tweens body sagged, confusion shifting into white-hot rage. "What... what is this?!" The voice was that of a elementary school aged girl, but the venom was pure Darius. He looked down at his smaller hands, panic spiking across his borrowed features.

Keesha pressed a hand to her mouth, tears brimming. Grace is in his body... Darius is in hers. She'd never truly believed a body-swap was possible until this moment.

Rodriguez, stunned, raised her radio. "We have a… situation," she managed, voice shaky. Officers had begun storming the house, guns drawn. They paused at the sight of the man they knew as Darius King standing uncertainly, arms lifted in confusion.

The Sirens Arrive

The storm continued to rage, wind lashing at the open door. Rain spattered the floor. Several uniformed officers rushed in, forming a perimeter. Red and blue lights flickered through the rain-swept darkness.

"Hands where we can see them!" one officer barked at the man they presumed to be Darius. Grace—inside Darius's body—lifted her arms, fear crossing her face. "Wait—no, I'm Grace!" she cried, voice trembling with that unfamiliar baritone. But the officers only heard Darius King's voice, recognized his face.

Darius, trapped in Grace's diminutive form, screeched, "You idiots! I'm Darius King! I'm the one you want!" But the officers saw only a panicked young girl. Some tried to calm her, while others focused on cuffing the man they believed was the real threat.

Chaos and Confusion

In the swirling confusion, Keesha fought to reach her daughter—her daughter now inhabiting a grown man's body. "Stop! That's not Darius!" she cried, pointing to the adult figure. "He's… that's my daughter! Please, let me explain!"

But the officers were trained to see Darius King as the prime suspect. They secured him first, slapping cuffs on his wrists. Grace bit her lip, trying not to resist, terror in her eyes. Over and over, she whispered, "Mom… Mom… please help…"

Meanwhile, the tweener's body that housed Darius flailed at the officers. "This is insane!" he yelled, voice cracking in a high pitch. He tried to exert psychic control, but nothing happened—no illusions, no forced compliance. He was helpless in a body that lacked the powers of his original form.

The Perfect Legal Snare

Rodriguez, struggling to maintain order, waved her badge, demanding the officers stand down. It was too late to prevent the immediate arrests; they'd seen the man they believed to be Darius. The real Darius, though physically a ten year old girl, was merely treated as a volatile minor.

Keesha's mind spun at the irony: Darius had orchestrated countless illusions, used his psychic might to dominate others, yet now found himself powerless in a frail, unfamiliar form. Grace had inadvertently created a perfect trap—so perfect it ensnared her too.

Quincy guided Keesha aside, letting the cops do their job. She trembled, tears streaming, as she watched them drag away the man—her real daughter, inside him—and subdue the young girl, who was actually Darius King. "We'll fix this," Quincy murmured, voice rough. "We'll find a way."

Aftermath and Resolutions

The storm raged, thunder rattling the shattered door. One officer hurried to pull it closed against the torrential downpour. Others secured the perimeter, checking each room for additional threats. Paramedics arrived, assessing for injuries, baffled by the bizarre tableau.

Keesha sank into the couch, feeling numb, while Rodriguez crouched beside her. "We'll sort out the identities," the detective promised, though her own eyes shone with uncertainty. "DNA tests, medical records—there must be a way to prove Grace isn't who she appears to be."

A wave of exhaustion crashed over Keesha. All her life, she had dreamed of a day when Darius was truly disarmed. Now he was—locked inside Grace's adolescent body, stripped of his psychic powers. Yet the cost was almost unbearable: Grace was trapped in his form, likely facing legal consequences as "Darius King."

Quincy put a steadying hand on Keesha's shoulder. "Look at it this way," he said softly. "Darius can't hurt anyone from inside Grace's body now. He has no power there."

Keesha swallowed hard, eyes flicking to the paramedics leading the "girl" away. Darius's voice came out as a frantic, adolescent wail. "You have to believe me! I'm Darius King!" The paramedics tried to soothe him, certain he was just a traumatized kid in shock.

Grace, in Darius's body, was gently pushed into the back of a squad car. Her wide eyes met Keesha's through the window. She mouthed, Help me.

A Mother's Resolve

Tears slipping down her cheeks, Keesha approached the car, placing a trembling hand on the glass. She mouthed back, I will. They locked gazes for a moment, mother and daughter still connected despite the bizarre switch that had stolen Grace's identity. Keesha forced a nod. Even in this chaos, she vowed to do whatever it took to restore Grace to her rightful body and finally neutralize Darius's threat.

Rodriguez conferred with the officers, instructing them to handle the "minor" with caution, no outside contact allowed. Keesha overheard scraps of conversation about possible mental health holds for the frantic prepubescent "Grace." Darius, she corrected in her mind.

Lightning flashed again, and Keesha winced at the thunder. She felt the house around her— battered, full of bullet holes and broken doors— reflecting the war they'd fought. They had won in one sense: Darius's power was undone. But the victory came at a steep price.

Outside, as the squad cars pulled away—one carrying Grace in Darius's form, the other carrying the outraged ten year old Darius—Keesha stepped into the pounding rain. Quincy rushed after her with an umbrella, but she waved it off. The cold water soaked her hair, plastering her clothes to her skin. She barely noticed. Her heart hammered, mind churning with next steps:

- Prove Grace's true identity.
- Keep Darius trapped in a body that lacked his powers.
- Or reverse the possession—risking a return of Darius's unstoppable psychic might?

Quincy and Rodriguez joined her on the porch, sharing the same unspoken question: What do we do now?

A Flicker of Hope

In the driving rain, Keesha closed her eyes, inhaling the petrichor. She recalled how Grace had said she felt Darius like a "beast in a cage." Perhaps that was still true—only now, he was the one caged in Grace's body. Maybe they could keep him there, powerless, while freeing Grace from being seen as a dangerous convict.

Across the street, neighbors peered from behind drawn curtains, alarmed by the police lights and the chaos. Keesha realized they must look like the aftermath of a disaster movie—shell-shocked, drenched in rain and heartbreak. But we're still standing, she reminded herself. We're still fighting.

She turned to Rodriguez, forcing the tremor from her voice. "Whatever it takes, Detective," she said. "We'll get Grace back in her own body without giving him back his power. Promise me you'll help us."

Rodriguez nodded resolutely, water dripping from the brim of her jacket. "I promise." There was steel in her eyes, even as uncertainty darkened them. "We'll find a way."

Coda: The Quiet After the Storm

Eventually, the police vehicles departed. The paramedics left. The house was empty except for Keesha, Quincy, and the echoing storm. The broken door, battered by wind, hung precariously on twisted hinges. A bullet lodged in the wall. The living room furniture overturned in the scramble.

Keesha sank onto the couch, shoulders shaking, tears finally unloosed. Quincy sat beside her, his arm around her back. A hush descended, punctuated by the rolling thunder overhead.

For once, it felt like the walls themselves were breathing with them, trying to process the impossible reversal they'd just witnessed. Their enemy was powerless—but so was their daughter, trapped in a body not her own.

Quincy gently wiped the rain from Keesha's cheek. "We'll make this right," he whispered, more to convince himself than her.

Keesha nodded. A kernel of triumph glowed deep in her chest: Grace had outsmarted Darius at his own game. Whatever came next, that fact remained. Her daughter was stronger than he'd ever believed. And perhaps that strength would guide them through the trials ahead—trials that would challenge everything they thought they knew about justice, identity, and the boundaries of reality.

Outside, the storm began to lessen, thunder moving off into the distance. Keesha rested her forehead against Quincy's shoulder, letting the tension slowly drain. Tomorrow, she'd have to face a fractured legal system that wouldn't believe a child could be trapped in a criminal's body. She'd have to fight for Grace in ways she never imagined. But for tonight, she allowed herself a single thought:

Darius wanted Grace for her mind, but she took his body instead. In a twisted irony, that might be the only way to keep him caged for good.

Lightning arced one last time, illuminating the living room in stark lines of white. Then the house fell into near-darkness, the storm's roar replaced by a soft patter of rain. Keesha breathed out, feeling the weight of countless battles. At least for now, Darius couldn't control their thoughts or illusions. They had severed his psychic might. That reality would have to be enough to sustain her through the uncertain dawn to come.

Chapter 5: The Fault Lines

The Weight of Two Realities

Keesha had never felt so torn. On the one hand, she was almost jubilant—Darius was, at last, powerless, trapped in a young girl's body that law enforcement treated as a minor in crisis rather than the monstrous manipulator he was. On the other hand, guilt sliced at her every thought. Her daughter, Grace, had paid the price by forfeiting her own form, occupying the body of the very man who'd terrorized them both.

She caught herself at random moments, pressing her fingers against her temple as if trying to quell a migraine that was more emotional than physical. Sometimes it felt surreal—like they had stepped into a science fiction plot, where minds swapped bodies in an unbelievable twist. But this was their life now, the constant hum of dread amplified by a legal system that couldn't make sense of the impossible.

Treading Legal Quicksand

Detective Elena Rodriguez juggled an impossible load. She kept telling Keesha, "We'll sort this out," but the detective's pinched expression betrayed her uncertainty. On paper, the body that appeared to be Darius King was not Darius at all—it bore physical evidence of Grace's unique medical history: a transplanted heart from her earlier surgeries, rods in the spine from scoliosis treatments, and a scattering of surgical scars that didn't match Darius's records.

Meanwhile, the real Darius—stranded in Grace's petite frame—fumed in juvenile detention. He screamed to anyone who would listen that he was "really" Darius King, and that the six-foot man in the hospital was a fraud. The staff, thoroughly disturbed by his outbursts, chalked it up to a severe delusional disorder. No one believed him. He was powerless, and ironically, that should have been cause for celebration.

But Rodriguez had the unenviable job of bridging this legal quagmire with the supernatural truth. What do we even charge the man we're calling Darius King with? the courts asked, when his physical body bore no sign of his original identity. How can this young girl be a notorious criminal? Keesha knew they were only scratching the surface of confusion.

Endless Days, Sleepless Nights

Keesha's routine became a loop of pacing between the hospital hallway and her living room. At the hospital, Grace (in Darius's body) underwent test after test, stumping medical professionals who found it "inexplicable" that this hulking adult male matched a ten year old girl's patient files. Doctors performed DNA analyses, expecting them to solve the puzzle. But the results caused more questions: The body belongs to Darius King, so why do we see evidence of Grace's medical journey?

Back home, Keesha tried to coax some semblance of normalcy out of the battered house, but it was impossible. Every time she entered the room where Grace (still in Darius's form) slept, she felt a spike of disorientation. Seeing that familiar crocheted blanket draped over a body that wore Darius's features—broad shoulders, scarred forearms—made her stomach turn. How did we get here?

Late nights blurred into early mornings. She'd catnap on the couch, haunted by the memory of Darius's twisted grin and Grace's panicked eyes. Then she'd wake with a jolt, heart pounding, uncertain if the body-swap was a dream or a nightmare made real. Each time, the reality slammed into her: they were truly living in a world turned upside down.

Grace's Inner Turmoil

For Grace, the shift was infinitely more harrowing. The relief of neutralizing Darius's psychic power warred with a profound sense of identity loss. She found herself startled by her own reflection: a tall, muscular man with stubble shadowing the jaw. Sometimes she'd catch a glimpse of herself in the bathroom mirror and recoil, mind reeling with memories of how that face used to sneer at her, how that voice once spat threats and commands.

On especially bad nights, Grace woke in a cold sweat, feeling as though she was still battling Darius in her dreams. She'd peel away the covers and stare down at hands that were not her own, thick fingers scarred from old injuries she never suffered. A jolt of revulsion made her shiver: It's his body. All the times I feared his touch, now it's me wearing his flesh.

Physically, she struggled with the differences— simple tasks like walking through a doorway became exercises in caution. She bumped her head on the lintel more than once, misjudging her new height. Dressing was awkward; none of her old clothes fit, and wearing Darius's old clothes—left behind in a closet—felt like stepping into the role of her worst nightmare. Even eating was strange, as she found herself with a ravenous appetite she never had before. The entire experience forced her to confront a question that gnawed at her: If my body defines so much of how I move, speak, and even feel hunger, is my soul the only thing that's really mine anymore?

The Silent Rock: Quincy

Quincy tried to be a quiet pillar of support for both mother and daughter, but the situation taxed even his steady composure. He grappled with a range of emotions—triumph that Darius no longer posed a psychic threat, rage at the universe for making Grace pay this devastating price, and guilt that he couldn't do more to shield her.

He often found Grace sitting on the edge of the bed, hunched in Darius's form, trying to remember how to coordinate limbs that felt so alien. Quincy would step in, demonstrating stances from his military training—ways to balance her weight, reduce clumsy collisions with furniture. He kept his tone pragmatic and gentle, never letting pity seep through.

> "Keep your center of gravity low," he'd coach softly. "Move from the hips, not just the shoulders. That way, you won't slam into door frames."

The first time Grace managed to walk from the living room to the kitchen without bashing her elbow, she let out a trembling laugh of relief. Quincy tried to return the smile, though it was tinged with sorrow. No one should have to relearn how to walk because she's trapped in her own abuser's body.

Dilemmas Piling High

All the while, practical concerns snowballed:

1. Proving Grace's Innocence: If they publicly admitted a mind-swap, the courts might dismiss them as delusional. Yet any standard approach—like releasing "Darius" because medical records showed he wasn't truly him—risked letting Darius slip back into a position where he could reclaim his original body.

2. Preventing Darius's Manipulations: Even if Darius was stuck in Grace's shell, no one could guarantee he wouldn't sweet-talk or manipulate the juvenile system. Already, Rodriguez heard rumors of staff members sympathizing with the "troubled girl," unwittingly giving him small freedoms.
3. Facing Permanence: The darkest question of all lingered in Keesha's mind: What if we can't swap them back? Could Grace spend the rest of her life in the body of a man who once haunted her nightmares?

Night of Revelation

One evening, well past midnight, Keesha found Grace in the living room, hunched over her sketchbook beneath the dim glow of a single lamp. The pages looked different—once filled with detailed, delicate pencil work, they now showcased heavy, bold lines of charcoal. Swirls of black conveyed something raw and tumultuous. It was as if she were drawing psychic storms, shapes that twisted and converged, reminiscent of the mental battle she'd waged against Darius.

Keesha quietly approached, heart aching at the way Grace's large shoulders dwarfed the small couch cushion. She placed a tentative hand on that muscular shoulder, still jarred by its solidity. "Baby, you've been so quiet," she said softly.

Grace set down her charcoal stick with a shaky breath. "I feel… disconnected. Like these drawings are from another life. I remember making them, but now it's like I'm peering at someone else's art."

She held up a page of slender, graceful lines— clearly from before the swap. "Those hands aren't mine anymore, Mom," she whispered. Her newly deepened voice wavered. "I look at my reflection, and sometimes all I see is him. I'm scared I'm… losing who I was."

Tears pricked Keesha's eyes. She crouched beside Grace, ignoring the mismatch in their sizes. "You could never lose who you are. Your essence isn't defined by your body or your face." Yet she felt a pang of doubt. Could repeated days, weeks, or months in Darius's body corrode Grace's sense of self?

Grace closed her eyes, tears slipping down cheeks that once belonged to Darius. "Thanks,

Mom," she murmured, voice catching. Then, opening them, she asked the question that had hovered between them for days: "When you look at me… do you see me, or do you see him?"

The rawness of the question cut deep. Keesha forced herself to hold Grace's gaze. "I see you," she said firmly. "But I won't lie—sometimes it's startling. I'll catch a glimpse of you from the side, and for a split second, I'm back in those nightmares. But then I remember: you're Grace, and I'd recognize you anywhere."

They fell silent, the hush thick with shared grief. Keesha longed to hold Grace the way she used to—pulling a lanky tween into her arms, tucking her head under her chin. Now, Grace was taller, broader, a shape that felt alien under her touch. But the bond was still there, intangible and fierce.

Echoes of the Past

When Grace finally drifted off to a restless sleep on the couch, Keesha remained awake, lost in memories. She remembered the first time she held Grace as a baby—so tiny, so warm. It felt impossible that the same daughter now wore the body of the man who once kept them awake with terror. That memory mingled with guilt: I pushed Grace to fight him. Did I unknowingly push her into this fate?

Eventually, she sensed someone behind her. Turning, she found Quincy standing in the doorway, silent. His eyes traveled from Keesha to the slumbering man-shape on the couch. She recognized the conflict in Quincy's gaze—relief that Darius no longer threatened them psychically, combined with anger that Grace had paid such a price.

"Couldn't sleep either?" Keesha whispered, voice hollow.

He shook his head, crossing the room to gently drape a blanket over Grace's broad shoulders. "Every time I close my eyes, I see her face when it used to be hers," he admitted. "I know how twisted that sounds, but I miss… her smile."

Keesha nodded, tears threatening. "Me too."

Glimpses of the Future

In the coming days, they would wrestle with doctors demanding explanations, with lawyers perplexed by contradictory evidence, with reporters sniffing around a high-profile case that "didn't add up." Yet the three of them—Keesha, Grace, and Quincy—clung to each other like castaways on a raft, determined not to let the swirling chaos tear them apart.

Rodriguez worked tirelessly to arrange private medical evaluations. She cornered forensics experts and psychiatrists, pushing for ways to prove that the adult body was truly Grace. Some suggested unprecedented "brain mapping," looking for anomalies that might match Grace's known patterns. But each day without resolution chipped away at Grace's sense of identity, leaving her wondering if she'd ever see her own reflection again.

Fragile Solidarity

Despite the confusion, a peculiar kind of solidarity grew between them. Keesha and Quincy rallied around Grace, encouraging her to share every fear, every pang of discomfort. They insisted she keep drawing, even if the art came out grim or chaotic. It was a tether to who she'd always been—a creative soul, forging beauty from the darkest corners.

Late one afternoon, Grace—fidgeting in a men's hoodie and sweatpants that still reeked of

Darius's aftershave—mustered a half-smile at Quincy's corny joke. Keesha's heart lifted at the sight. It was small, but it was progress.

> "You're still in there," Keesha thought, watching Grace manage a gentle laugh. "No matter how different you look, you're still the kid who used to chase fireflies in the yard."

The Unspoken Truth

In stolen, vulnerable moments, each of them acknowledged what they couldn't say out loud: If Darius somehow managed to break free, if he reclaimed his original body or discovered a new psychic trick, they might be back to square one—or worse. A swirl of moral questions haunted them:

- Could they ethically keep Darius trapped in Grace's shell forever, just to ensure his powers never returned?
- Would Grace be forced to remain in a man's body indefinitely, sacrificing her own identity for the greater good?
- Or was there a way to swap them back that wouldn't restore Darius's monstrous abilities?

No one had the answers, and the uncertainty gnawed at them like a slow, relentless tide.

A Flicker of Hope

Toward the end of one long, exhausting day, Keesha found Grace staring at the door that led to the backyard. Beyond it lay a small patch of grass where Grace used to practice drawing birds, or just lounge under the sun. She turned to Keesha, eyes brimming with sorrow. "I want to feel the sunlight again," she said. "I've been cooped up in hospitals and the living room, hiding behind curtains. I'm tired of feeling like I don't belong in my own life."

Keesha swallowed hard, tears pricking her eyes. "Let's go out," she whispered. "At least for a little while, okay?" And so they did, stepping into the late afternoon glow, ignoring the stares of neighbors who might see the tall man leaning on Keesha's arm.

They sat quietly on the back steps, the sun warming Grace's unfamiliar skin. A breeze rustled the overgrown grass. For a moment, Keesha could almost pretend nothing had changed—the day was calm, the sky an open blue. Grace even closed her eyes, breathing deeply, letting the fresh air fill her lungs.

"We'll figure this out," Keesha said softly, placing a hand over Grace's large, calloused palm. "I promise."

Grace opened her eyes, a faint smile ghosting her lips. "I know," she murmured. Despite the borrowed timbre of her voice, Keesha heard her daughter's honesty. "We got this far. We won't give up now."

Uncharted Tomorrows

The promise of tomorrow hung heavy in the air. Darius, confined in a juvenile ward, raged helplessly. The courts and doctors floundered. But in that back yard, Keesha felt a fragile surge of hope. Grace had outmatched Darius in the psychic realm once. Perhaps, with enough determination and loyalty, they could find a way to restore her body without unleashing the monster again.

Their future balanced on a precarious fault line, where love and guilt, relief and anxiety, all swirled together. Yet as mother and daughter leaned into each other's presence—no matter how mismatched their outward forms—one truth shone clear: They hadn't lost each other. Grace was still Grace, Keesha was still her mother, and together, with Quincy's unwavering support, they would brace against the uncertain horizon, refusing to let Darius or fate tear them apart.

Chapter 6: The Aftermath

A Rain-Soaked Dawn

Dawn arrived beneath a slate-gray sky, a gentle drizzle washing over a neighborhood too accustomed to late-night sirens and whispered rumors. Keesha stood at the kitchen window, watching raindrops race each other down the glass. Outside, the world looked almost peaceful, but she couldn't ignore the faint smell of gunpowder residue lingering from recent chaos. The house itself bore fresh scars: bullet holes in the walls, splintered door frames, and the stale chemical tang of medical disinfectant left behind by Dr. Flores's late-night visits.

A wry thought flickered through Keesha's mind: How many times have we tried to patch these walls, only to see them torn open again? The absurdity almost drew a laugh from her, but she held it in, knowing it would sound hollow in the silent morning. She glanced down at her hands. Even after all these months of crisis, they still trembled whenever a car door slammed too loudly outside.

New Routines in a Shaken World

In the living room, Grace moved with cautious steps, testing her balance in a body that felt like it belonged to someone else. That was because, in the most literal sense, it did. She wore Darius's towering form like an ill-fitting suit— heavy muscles, broad shoulders, height that forced her to duck under the ceiling fan if she stood on tiptoe. Each time she bumped into furniture, her face twisted in frustration. She used to know this house intimately, every nook and cranny, but her newfound size and unfamiliar muscle memory made it all feel off-kilter.

Quincy, methodical as ever, was in the process of repairing the broken door. Every hammer strike sent a sharp echo through the halls, resonating like a reminder of the previous night's violence. He paused every so often to wipe sweat from his brow or adjust his grip, glancing over at Grace with a mixture of quiet concern and pride.

They had all settled into a strangely intimate routine in under twenty-four hours:

- Keesha brewed coffee at the crack of dawn, hoping the aroma might mask the lingering smell of anxiety in the air.
- Grace walked laps around the living room, trying not to knock over side tables that once stood at her waist but now came up to her knees.
- Quincy reminded them to breathe, to unclench their fists and jaws, gently insisting the worst was over. Or so they hoped.

The Precinct's Grim Updates

By mid-morning, Detective Elena Rodriguez arrived, looking grave. Her shoulders carried the weight of a legal system that wasn't built to handle a mind-swap. She laid out new developments from the precinct, describing how Darius—still trapped in Grace's body—ranted about "identity theft" and demanded an audience with higher officials. Most brushed the claims off as the delusions of a traumatized minor. But a few suspected deeper manipulation at play. No one in the legal system was prepared to accept the notion that two people had literally traded bodies.

Yet, enough people trusted Rodriguez's instincts to keep Darius (in Grace's body) under strict observation. She told them how some staff members pitied the "troubled girl," wanting to help her recover from supposed psychological trauma. Others took a more cautious approach, suspecting manipulation tactics. "He's locked down," Rodriguez reassured them, "but we have to stay vigilant. He's wily, even without his powers."

Dr. Flores's Revelations

Soon after, Dr. Miriam Flores arrived, dark circles under her eyes betraying sleepless nights spent analyzing medical scans. She spread new test results across the dining table, pointing out obvious markers that once belonged to Grace: a transplanted heart, the subtle rods and fusions from scoliosis surgeries, the faint scarring on the lungs. These were unmistakable signatures that Grace had lived in this body—except now, that body physically appeared to be Darius King.

"This confirms," Dr. Flores said, "beyond any doubt, that the man the authorities have been calling 'Darius King' must have once been Grace. It's biologically impossible otherwise."

Keesha felt a fleeting surge of relief. Evidence—finally. Yet Dr. Flores's expression remained clouded. "But," she continued, "it doesn't prove the mind inside is really Grace. The courts might acknowledge a 'mistaken identity' on a surface level, but no judge will sign off on the possibility of a supernatural swap." She exhaled, frustration evident. "I'm doing what I can to give you legal breathing room."

Legal Forks in the Road

Quincy crossed his arms, his stance radiating protectiveness. "So what now?" he asked, voice low. "We use the medical evidence to argue that Grace—physically disguised as Darius—can't be held accountable for Darius's crimes?"

Dr. Flores nodded. "Precisely. With these scans, the District Attorney may drop or at least suspend charges against 'Darius King' pending more 'medical evaluations.' If that happens, Grace would be transferred out of standard custody, giving her some privacy and security."

Keesha felt her heart flutter with cautious hope. But she couldn't ignore the deeper problem. "And then what?" she asked, her voice trembling. "What about actually reversing the swap?"

A tense silence followed. Flores glanced at Grace, whose broad shoulders hunched defensively. "Replicating the same conditions that caused the swap is dangerous. It would involve a high-stakes psychic confrontation. If we tried it, we'd risk returning Darius to his original body—and unleashing his powers again. No one can predict the outcome."

Grace's Quiet War

Grace stood to the side, studying her new forearms as if they belonged to a stranger. She rubbed a hand over the thick cords of muscle, her face a mixture of unease and intrigue. "Could I live like this?" she murmured, half to herself. The question hung heavy in the air. Could she accept a permanent life in the body of the man who terrorized her? She wasn't sure she wanted to know the answer.

She remembered the sense of victory that flared when she'd turned Darius's own psychic assault against him, but that triumph soured whenever she caught sight of her reflection—a face she once saw only in nightmares. Even the strength she felt in these limbs was a constant reminder of Darius's physical dominance. At times, it almost felt like an invasion of her soul.

Tension on the Couch

After Rodriguez and Flores departed, night settled again over the battered house. Quincy dozed in a chair, pistol still within arm's reach, as if expecting Darius to burst in at any moment. The steady tick of an old clock punctuated the hush.

Keesha and Grace sat on the couch, the flicker of a lone table lamp highlighting the bullet holes in the wall. Grace leaned against her mother's shoulder, even though the bulk of her new frame made the gesture feel awkwardly reversed. For Keesha, the weight of Grace's body pressed against her was startling—heavy, solid—but there was a tenderness in how Grace nestled in, as if longing for the closeness of simpler times.

"Mom," Grace said quietly, the rumble of her voice still throwing Keesha off-guard. "I'm scared of... what I might become. If I'm stuck in his body long enough, do I start to... pick up pieces of him?"

Keesha felt her throat tighten. "He can't change who you are inside," she insisted, threading her fingers through Grace's short, rough hair. It was a reflex from years of comforting her child. "You stood up to him, Grace. You won. Don't you see? That's your strength."

The tears that slipped from Grace's eyes cut through Keesha's resolve, drawing her own tears to the surface. Grace had never looked more vulnerable, despite her imposing physique. Keesha wrapped her arms around Grace's broad shoulders, rocking gently. The role reversal wasn't lost on her—the "child" dwarfed the mother now, yet the dynamic was the same: Keesha, offering solace; Grace, seeking reassurance.

The Weight of Their Bonds

For a few minutes, mother and daughter simply wept together, each tear a lament for what had been lost: Grace's familiar body, any illusion of normalcy, and perhaps the hope that Darius could be neutralized without so much collateral damage. Yet in that same outpouring of grief, Keesha felt a fierce bond solidify within them. She realized that no matter what shape Grace wore, she would always be her daughter. Nothing would tear them apart.

Eventually, their tears subsided to soft sniffles. Grace pulled back, wiping her eyes with the back of a hand that felt rough and foreign to her. Keesha offered a small, sad smile, gently brushing a stray hair from Grace's forehead. "We've come this far," she whispered. "We won't abandon each other."

Quincy, half-awake in his chair, cleared his throat. "That's right," he murmured, as if in agreement, eyes still closed. Even dozing, he refused to leave them unguarded.

Reflections on the Night

Outside, the drizzle continued, painting the windows in silver rivulets. Streetlights glowed through the watery haze, giving the living room a moody ambiance. Keesha stared at the faint reflection of herself and Grace in the glass. She thought of all the battles they'd fought—of how Darius once controlled entire rooms of people with a thought. Now, ironically, he was locked in a juvenile ward, powerless.

But that victory was tangled with moral and existential dread:

- If they tried to reverse the swap, they might restore Darius's psychic might.
- If they allowed Grace to remain in his body, it could mean a lifetime of disassociation, loss, and public confusion.
- Meanwhile, the legal system demanded some plausible explanation, and the media might catch wind of "Darius King's bizarre transformation."

A Flicker of Determination

Yet somewhere amid the gloom, Keesha felt the flicker of a new determination. Grace was alive. Grace was free—at least from Darius's direct control. That meant there was hope, no matter how tangled the path might be. She'd do whatever it took to see her daughter find a future that felt like her own, whether in her original body or not.

A subtle strength rippled through her. This was the same grit that had carried her through the years of surviving Darius's manipulations, the same maternal ferocity that had helped them orchestrate the night they trapped him. If she needed to delve into the realm of the paranormal again, so be it. If she needed to stand before judges and doctors, brandishing bizarre truths like a banner, she would.

Contemplating Tomorrow's Battles

For now, though, exhaustion weighed on them all. Keesha pressed a soft kiss to Grace's temple, ignoring the scratch of stubble. "Let's get some sleep," she suggested. Grace nodded. With a gentle squeeze of her mother's hand, she rose from the couch—still mindful not to bang her head on the hanging light fixture—and made her way to the spare bedroom that had once been a storage space. It was the only bed that could comfortably fit her new frame.

Keesha lingered in the living room a moment longer, her eyes sweeping over the battered walls and the half-repaired door. The hush of the rain lulled her into a state of weary acceptance. We survived another day, she reminded herself, and we'll face tomorrow when it comes.

The Gray Quiet of Dawn

By the time morning crept up again, the rain had tapered to a faint drizzle, leaving the neighborhood in a misty cloak. This time, Keesha met the dawn with a steadier heart. She brewed coffee in the kitchen, determined not to let her trembling fingers spill it. Quincy emerged from the spare room, rolling his stiff shoulders as if preparing for a new mission.

Grace still slumbered, the exhaustion of her transformation weighing heavy. Keesha let her sleep. She ventured onto the porch, sipping her coffee while the sky softened from charcoal to pale silver. Cars occasionally rumbled by, neighbors quietly resuming their daily routines. For them, life went on. For Keesha, it felt like she stood on the edge of a great abyss, the future uncertain.

Yet one thing was certain: they were in this together. She inhaled the damp morning air, recalling Grace's trembling question the night before—What if there's some part of him that rubs off on me? She closed her eyes, reaffirming her resolve: He can't ever take what makes you you, my sweet girl. We won't let him.

Unanswered Questions

As the household woke and the day progressed, they knew more hurdles lay ahead:

- Darius's next court date or parole hearing.
- Medical evaluations that might or might not support Grace's claims.
- The possibility of exploring psychic means to restore her body, weighed against the terror of freeing Darius's powers.

They were living in a legal and moral labyrinth with no easy exits. But as Keesha prepared a simple breakfast—scrambled eggs and toast—she felt a spark of confidence. She, Grace, and Quincy had toppled Darius's stranglehold once. They'd find a way through this labyrinth, too.

Bonds Unbreakable

That evening, as dusk settled once more, mother and daughter found themselves side by side on the back step, listening to the distant hum of traffic and feeling the soft brush of a waning breeze. Grace turned her gaze skyward, scanning for stars through the thinning clouds. Her shoulders still looked too broad for a tweener's hoodie, her posture uncertain. But in the curve of her faint smile, Keesha glimpsed the child she'd raised.

> "We do not abandon each other," Keesha reminded her quietly.

Grace nodded, the corners of her eyes misting with gratitude. "Never."

The hush that enveloped them was poignant, laced with both sorrow for what had been lost and a fierce pride in what they had preserved. No matter what shape Grace's future took, Keesha vowed to stand by her side—shielding her from a world that refused to believe in the impossible and from a predator who would likely do anything to reclaim his power.

They had survived Darius's manipulations. They had broken his hold.

Yet the future glimmered with unknown perils:

- The threat of a possible reversal that might unleash Darius's psychic wrath.
- The choice of keeping him trapped at the cost of Grace's bodily autonomy.
- A legal labyrinth that demanded answers where none existed.

In that twilight hush, as the last of the rain dripped from the eaves, they clung to each other—two souls bound by love, defying the odds. It was not a perfect haven, but it was theirs. The promise thrummed like a heartbeat in the air: We will not abandon each other.

And that, they both knew, might be the strongest shield they had left.